Granny Dryden's Runaway Pig

Story by **John Cunliffe**

Pictures by **Ray Mutimer**

from the original Television designs by **Ivor Wood**

Hippo Books
Scholastic Publications Limited
London

Scholastic Publications Ltd.,
10 Earlham Street, London WC2H 9RX, UK

Scholastic Inc.,
730 Broadway, New York, NY 10003, USA

Scholastic Canada Ltd.,
123 Newkirk Road, Richmond Hill,
Ontario L4C 3G5, Canada

Ashton Scholastic Pty. Ltd.,
P O Box 579, Gosford, New South Wales,
Australia

Ashton Scholastic Ltd.,
165 Marua Road, Panmure, Auckland 6,
New Zealand

First published in hardback by André Deutsch Ltd., 1990
Published in paperback by Scholastic Publications Ltd., 1991

Text copyright © John Cunliffe, 1990

Illustration copyright © André Deutsch Ltd, Scholastic Publications Ltd and
Woodland Animations Ltd, 1990

ISBN 0 590 76418 7

Pat called at Greendale Farm on Saturday morning. Katy and Tom were busy. They had their paints and crayons out. Katy was drawing her new pony. Tom was drawing Katy.

"Do you know any drawing-stories?" said Pat.

"What?" said Tom.

"What kind of story is that?" said Katy.

"I'll show you," said Pat. "May I borrow your
crayon?"

Katy gave Pat a large crayon and some paper.

"You tell the story as you make the picture," said Pat. "I'll tell you the one about Granny Dryden and her pig."

Pat drew as he talked. This is what he drew, and this is what he said . . . .

"Granny Dryden used to keep a pig in her garden. It had a special house to sleep in. You can see it still, if you look round the back, just by the rhubarb-patch. She keeps her flower-pots there now. And it had a place of its own where it could run and rootle and roll in the mud, with a fence to keep it off the flowers.

It was a nice pig, but it *would* run away, given half a chance. Many's the time Ted and I have chased after it and brought it back for her. This time she went looking for it herself, but she didn't find it, because . . . well, you'll see what happened.

The latch had worked loose on the gate, but nobody had taken any notice. It was a windy day as well. Granny Dryden was too busy to notice what her pig was up to. She was busy making jam, and she was making a cake as well. Now what do you think she'd be wearing, to work in the kitchen?"

"An apron?" said Tom.

"That's right."

[Pat drew Granny Dryden's apron, like this . . .]

"What kind of cake was she making?" said Katy.

"A birthday-cake."

"Who was it for?" said Tom.

"It was for you and Katy!"

"*Delicious*," said Tom and Katy.

"I popped in with your card, asking her to come to
your party. She said, 'Hello, Pat! Would you put it on
the table, please? I'm too busy and too sticky to look
at it just now. And I haven't had time to put the kettle
on, so I cannot even offer you a cup of tea.'

'That's all right!' I said. 'I can see how busy you are. Dorothy Thompson's sure to be brewing up. I'll have a cup with her. See you tomorrow!

Cheerio!'

"And off I went, on my way with the letters. I made sure the gate was well closed, and the pig seemed to be asleep. But it wasn't! Granny Dryden told me the next day what happened.

"No sooner had I gone, than the wind blew that gate open, with its wobbly latch being so loose, and that naughty pig gave the gate an extra push, and away it went, over the hill as fast as it could go. Granny Dryden had to leave her cake half-made, and run after it. She ran out of the gate and over the hill.

[Pat drew the hill, next to the apron, like this . . .]

"And when she went over the hill, the wind blew, and the wind blew, and the wind blew, and it tangled up the ribbons on her apron, like this . . .

[Pat drew the tangled ribbons . . .]

"She couldn't see her pig anywhere, so on she went.
She said, 'I wonder if that silly pig has gone and
fallen down the well at Greendale Farm?'"

"That's our well," said Katy.

"Where you dropped your hat," said Tom.

"I know. Granny Dryden went round this way to look down the well, to see if she could see her pig . . .

[Pat drew the way she walked, and the well she looked down, like this . . .]

"But she couldn't see her pig."

"That looks like . . ." said Katy.

"Yes?"

"I'm not sure," said Katy.

"Hmmmmm . . . ." said Tom.

"And then Granny Dryden thought of the other well, down in the meadow, so she went to look down that, as well."

[Pat drew another well, like this . . .]

"It *is*," said Tom.

"I'm not sure," said Katy.

"Granny Dryden still could not see her pig. 'Where has that silly pig gone?' she said. But she went on.

She went through the valley . . .

[Pat drew the valley . . .]

"And then she slipped in a puddle. Down she went . . .

[Pat drew a line to show where she fell.]

"She got up. Then she slipped in *another* puddle. Down she went again!"

[Pat drew another place where she fell.]

"It is," said Katy and Tom together.

"She still could not see her pig. She went round the corner, and looked in the cave.

[Pat drew the mouth of a cave.]

"And all she could see was a round oil-drum with two holes in it."

[Pat drew the end of the oil-drum.]

Katy and Tom began to laugh, and shout, "A pig! A pig!"

But Pat went on with the story . . .

"Now Granny Dryden was tired. She turned for home.

'I'll put that cake in the oven,' she said, 'and I'll have a rest and a cup of tea, then I'll have another look for my naughty pig.'

"She went back up the steep hill, on the way home.

[Pat drew the way she went . . .]

"But when she got home, there, in the garden . . .

[Pat drew in the pig's eye.]

"... was her pig, waiting for his dinner! He had come home all by himself!"

Now the drawing and the story were finished. How the twins laughed and clapped their hands!

"I knew it was going to be a pig," said Tom.

"So did I," said Katy.

"Please," said Tom, "can I keep it?"

"Yes," said Pat, "but I'll draw another one for Katy."

And he did. They coloured them, and put them up on their bedroom wall.

They told the story again, when Dad came in for his tea. And, when friends, or aunts and uncles, come to visit, Katy and Tom draw and tell the story of Granny Dryden and her pig, just as Pat drew it for them. And so can you.